Eek & Ack
The Puzzling Pluto Plot

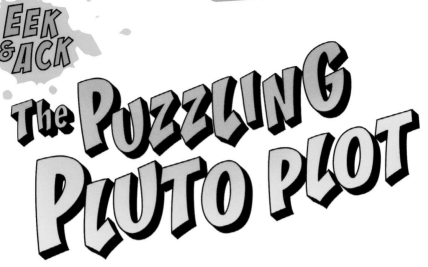

Librarian Reviewer
Katharine Kan
Graphic novel reviewer and Library Consultant, Panama City, FL
MLS in Library and Information Studies, University of Hawaii at Manoa, HI

Reading Consultant
Elizabeth Stedem
Educator/Consultant, Colorado Springs, CO
MA in Elementary Education, University of Denver, CO

STONE ARCH BOOKS
Minneapolis San Diego

Library of Congress Cataloging-in-Publication Data
Hoena, B. A.
    The Puzzling Pluto Plot / by Blake A. Hoena; illustrated by Steve Harpster.
    p. cm. — (Graphic Sparks—Eek and Ack)
    ISBN 978-1-4342-0452-3 (library binding)
    ISBN 978-1-4342-0502-5 (paperback)
    1. Graphic novels. I. Harpster, Steve. II. Title.
PN6727.H57P89 2008
741.5'973—dc22   2007031255

Summary: Eek and Ack aren't giving up! The Terrible Twosome from the Great Goo
Galaxy are out to conquer Earth once again. But maybe they should have studied up on
the solar system first. Let's just say, the "planet" Pluto will never be the same.

Art Director: Heather Kindseth
Graphic Designer: Brann Garvey

For Curt, who continues to believe
in Pluto's planetary status

Printed in the United States of America in Stevens Point, Wisconsin.
009964R

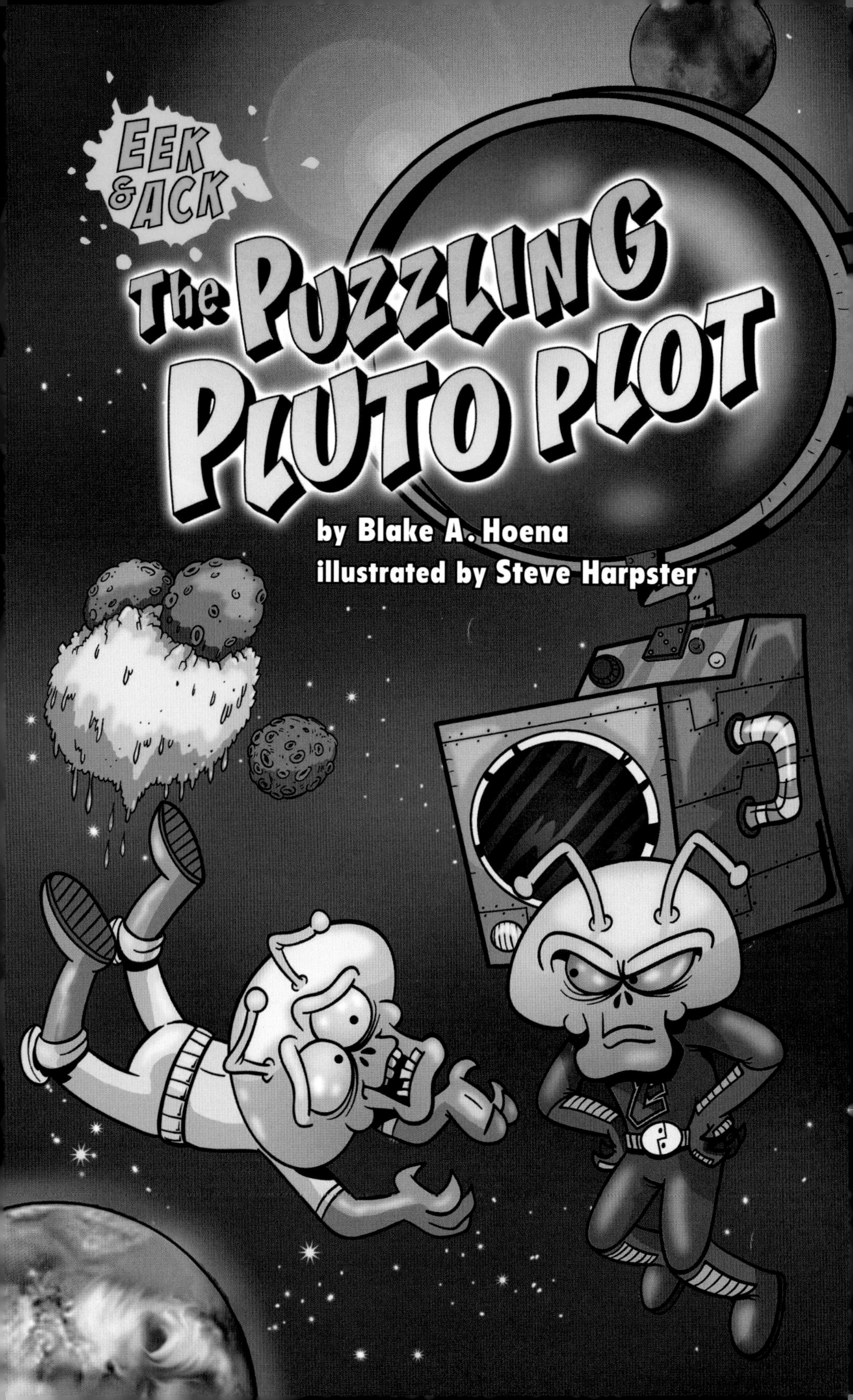
EEK & ACK
The PUZZLING PLUTO PLOT
by Blake A. Hoena
illustrated by Steve Harpster

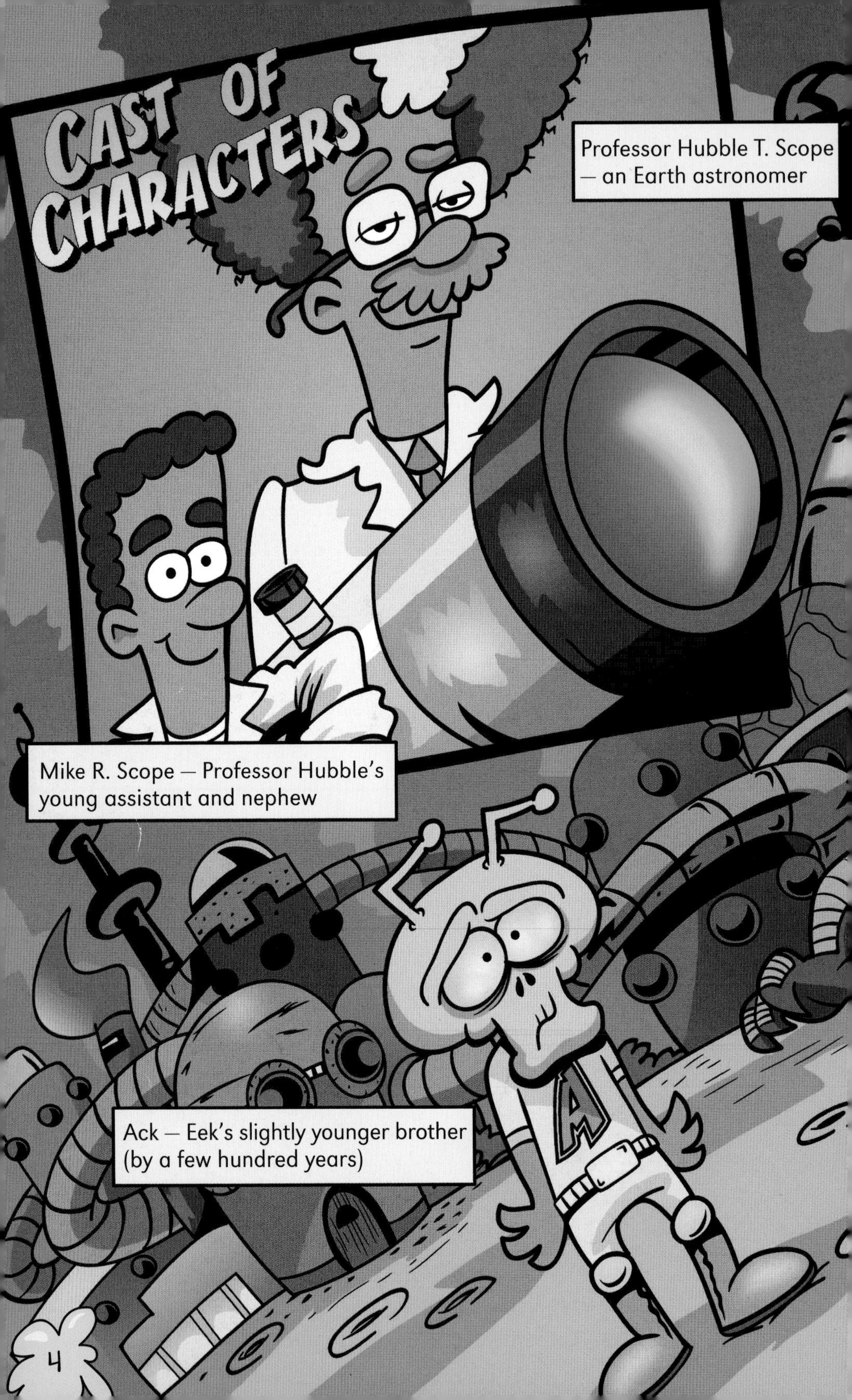
CAST OF CHARACTERS
Professor Hubble T. Scope — an Earth astronomer
Mike R. Scope — Professor Hubble's young assistant and nephew
Ack — Eek's slightly younger brother (by a few hundred years)

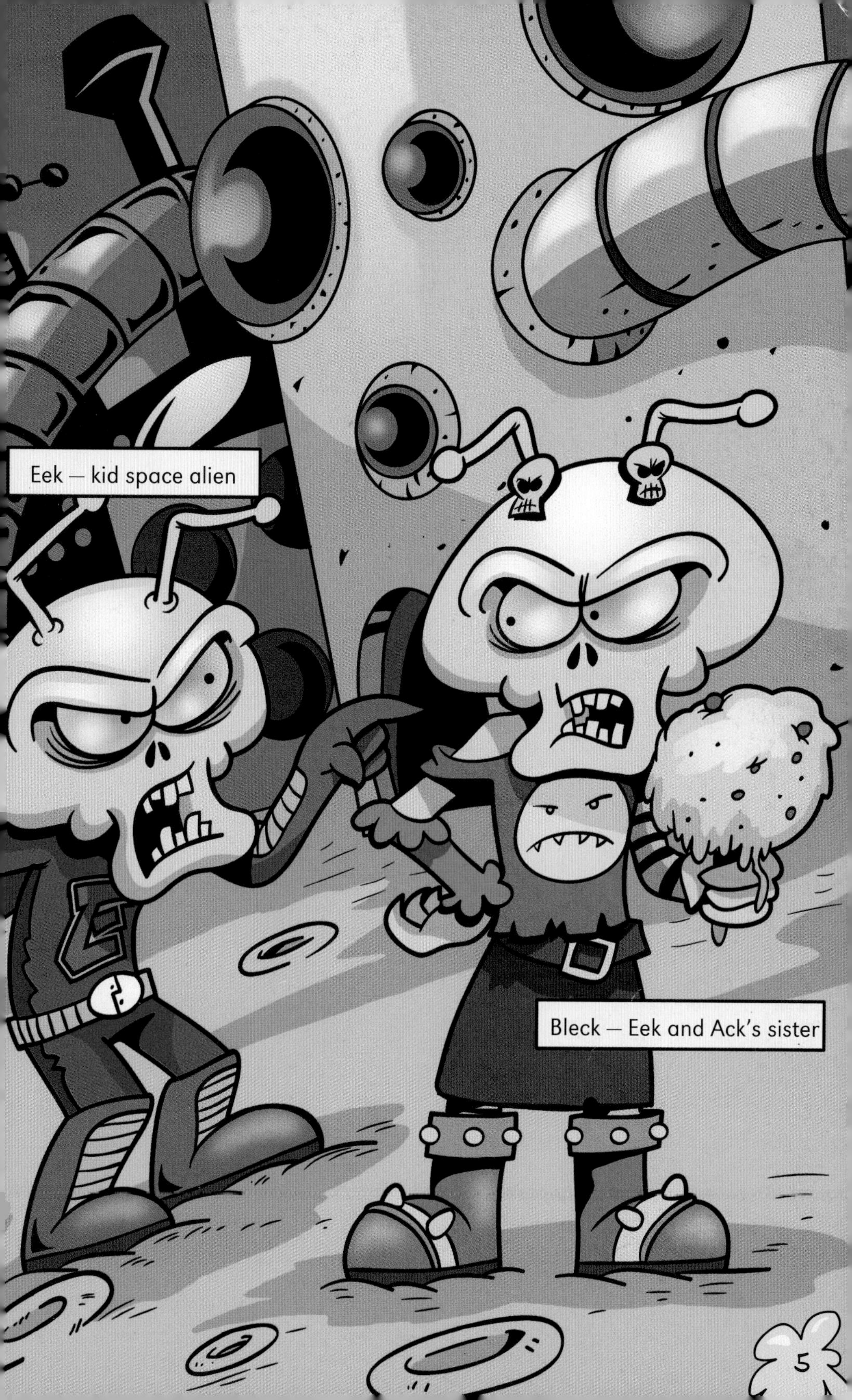
Eek — kid space alien
Bleck — Eek and Ack's sister

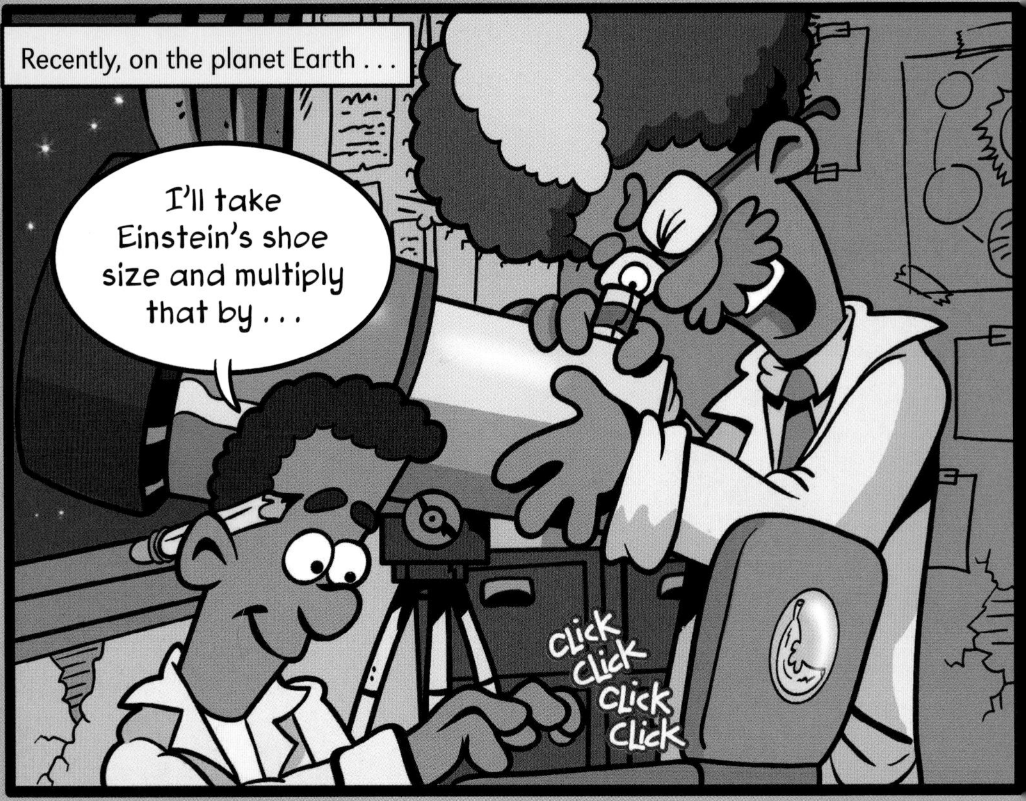
Recently, on the planet Earth . . .
I'll take Einstein's shoe size and multiply that by . . .
CLICK CLICK CLICK CLICK

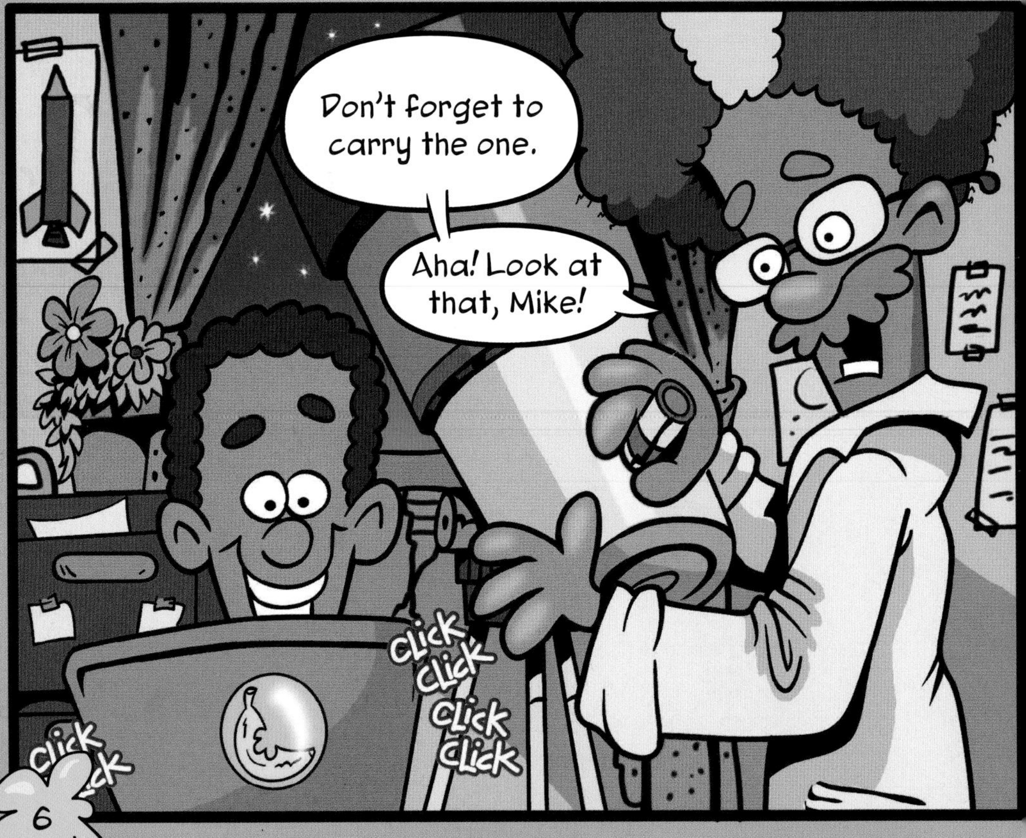
Don't forget to carry the one.
Aha! Look at that, Mike!
CLICK CLICK CLICK CLICK

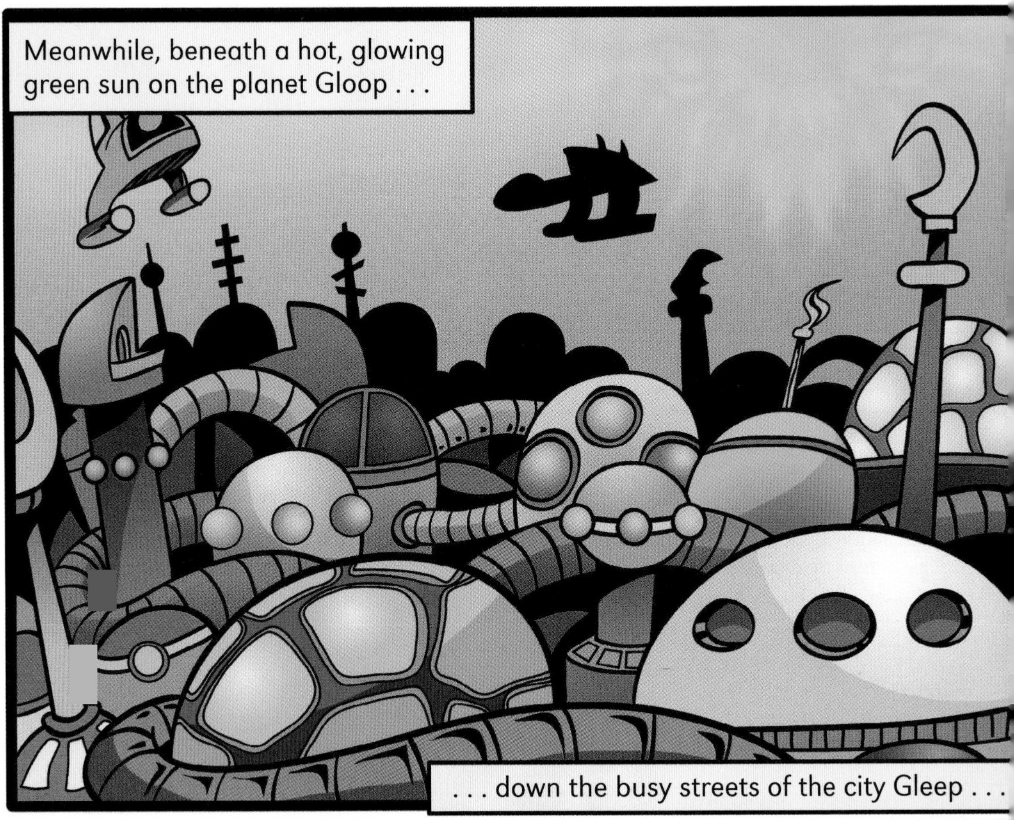
Meanwhile, beneath a hot, glowing green sun on the planet Gloop . . .
. . . down the busy streets of the city Gleep . . .

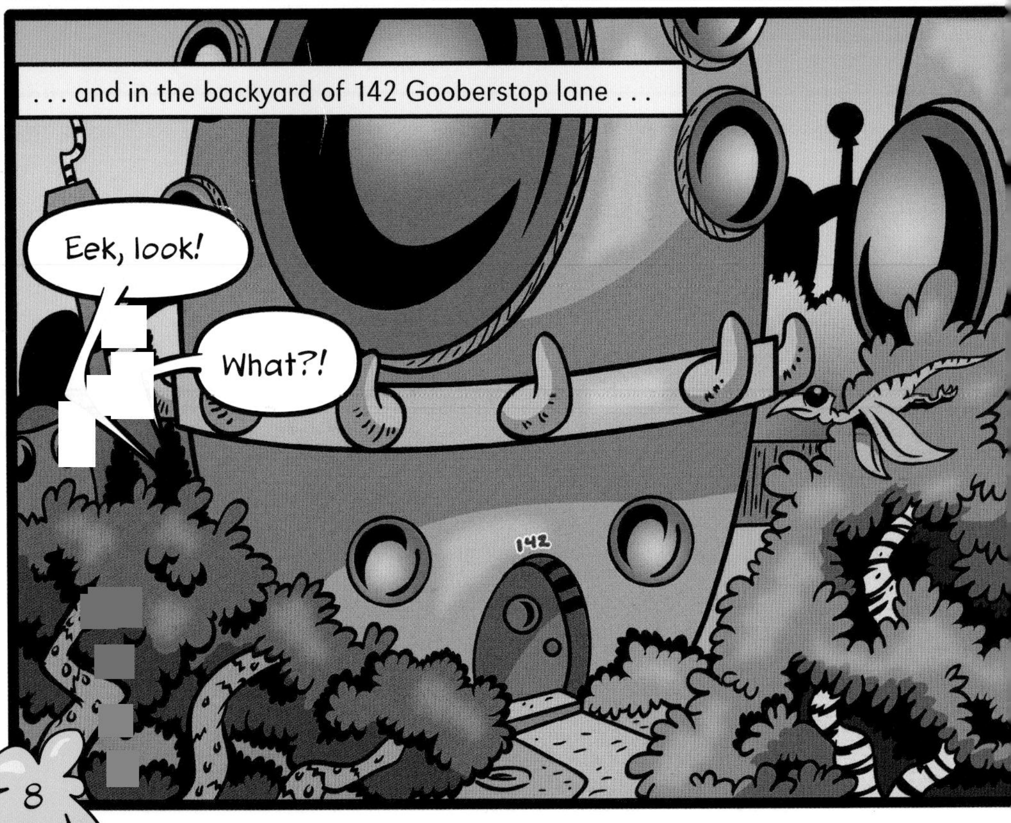
. . . and in the backyard of 142 Gooberstop lane . . .
Eek, look!
What?!
142

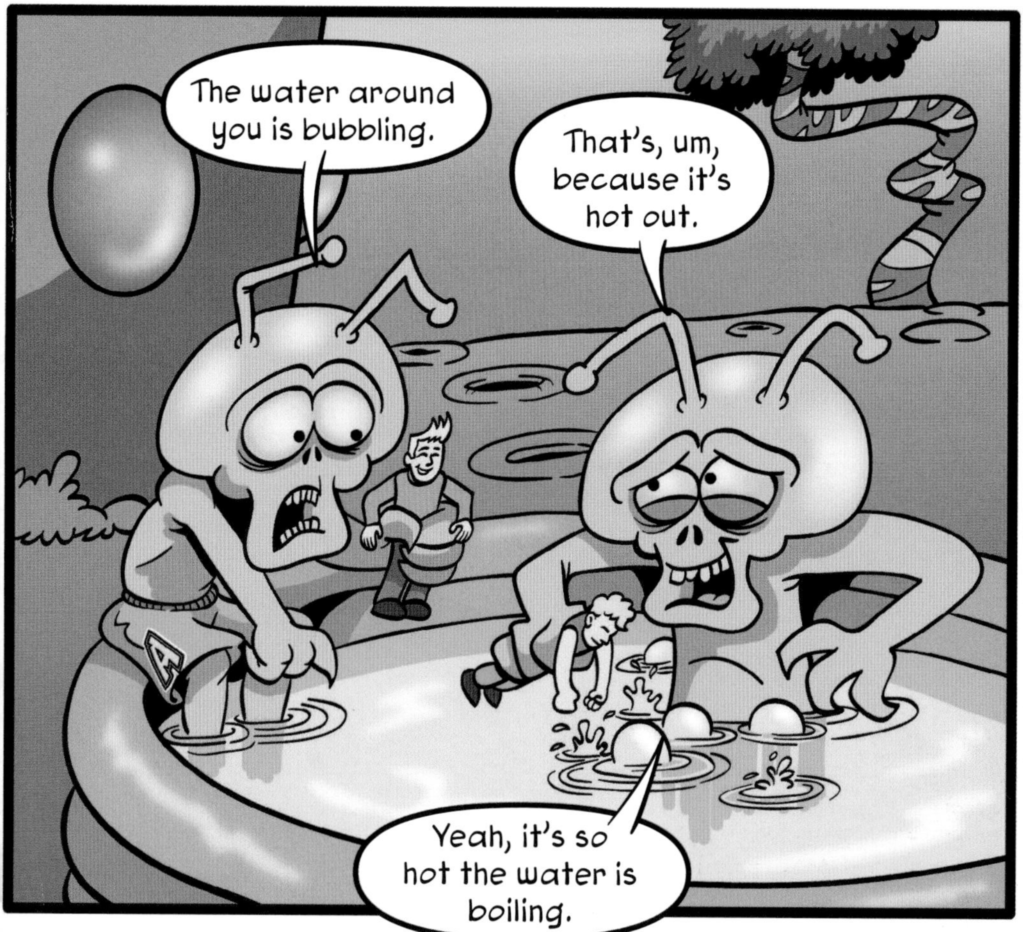
The water around you is bubbling.
That's, um, because it's hot out.
Yeah, it's so hot the water is boiling.

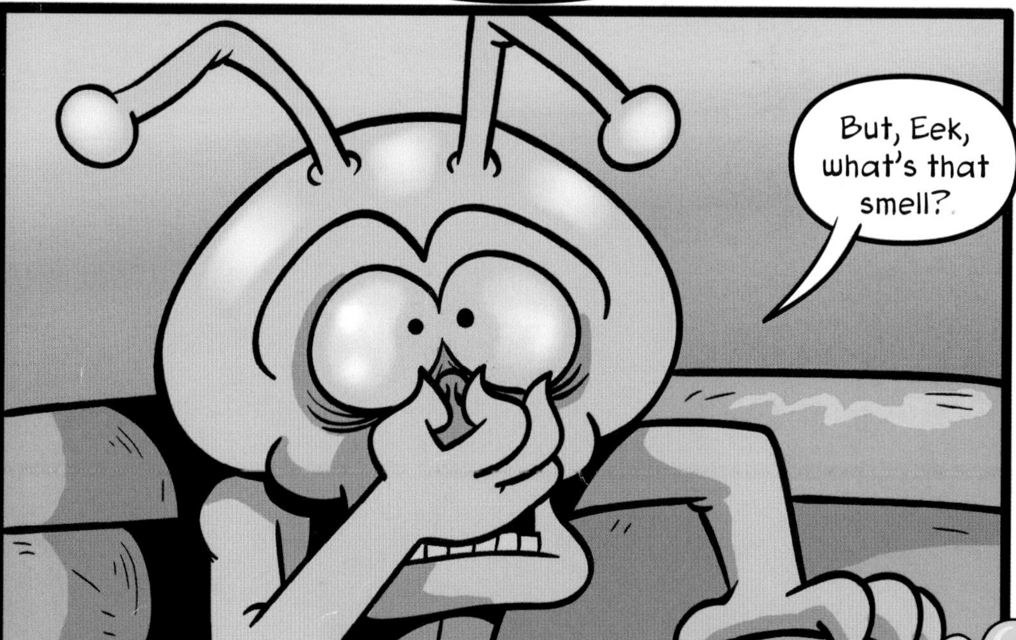
But, Eek, what's that smell?

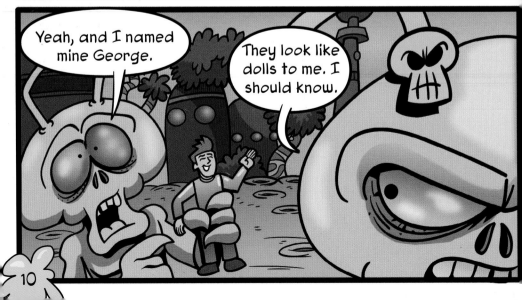

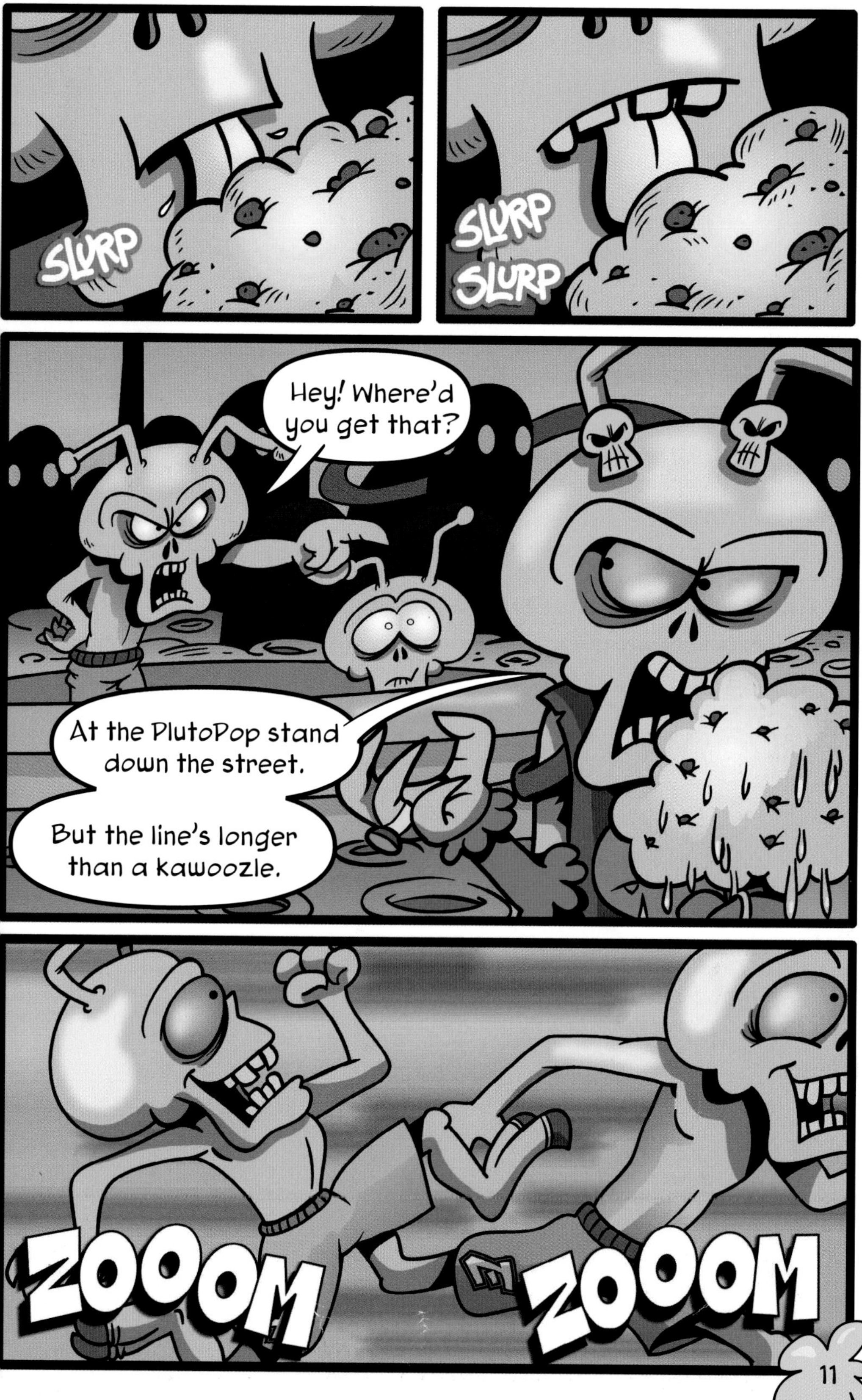
SLURP
SLURP
SLURP
Hey! Where'd you get that?
At the PlutoPop stand down the street.
But the line's longer than a kawoozle.
ZOOOM
ZOOOM

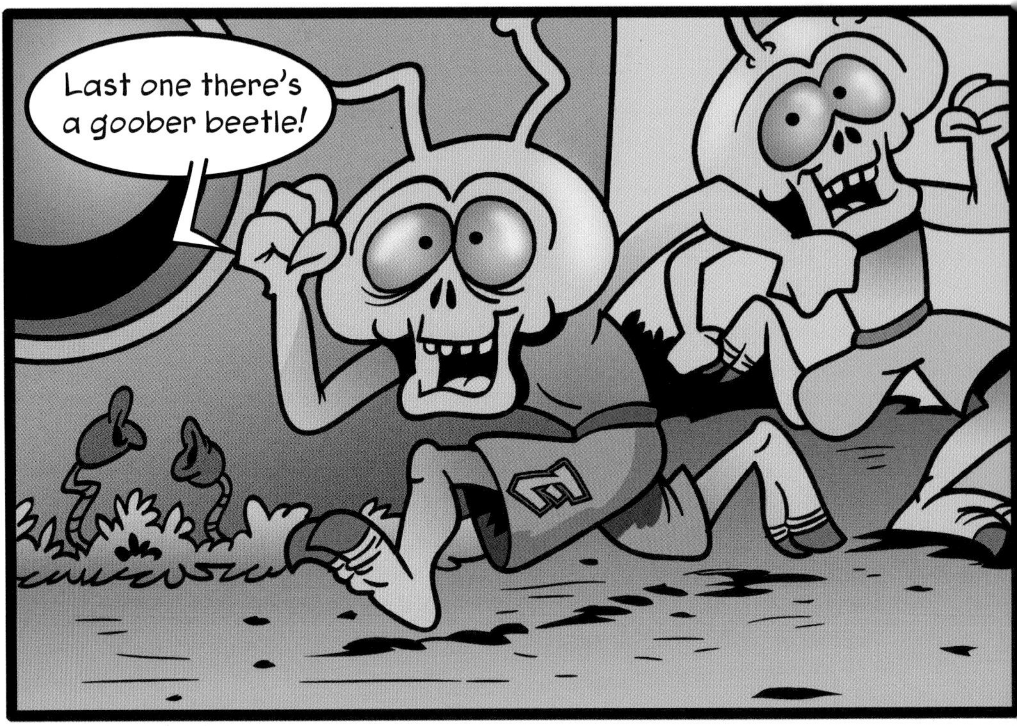
Last one there's a goober beetle!

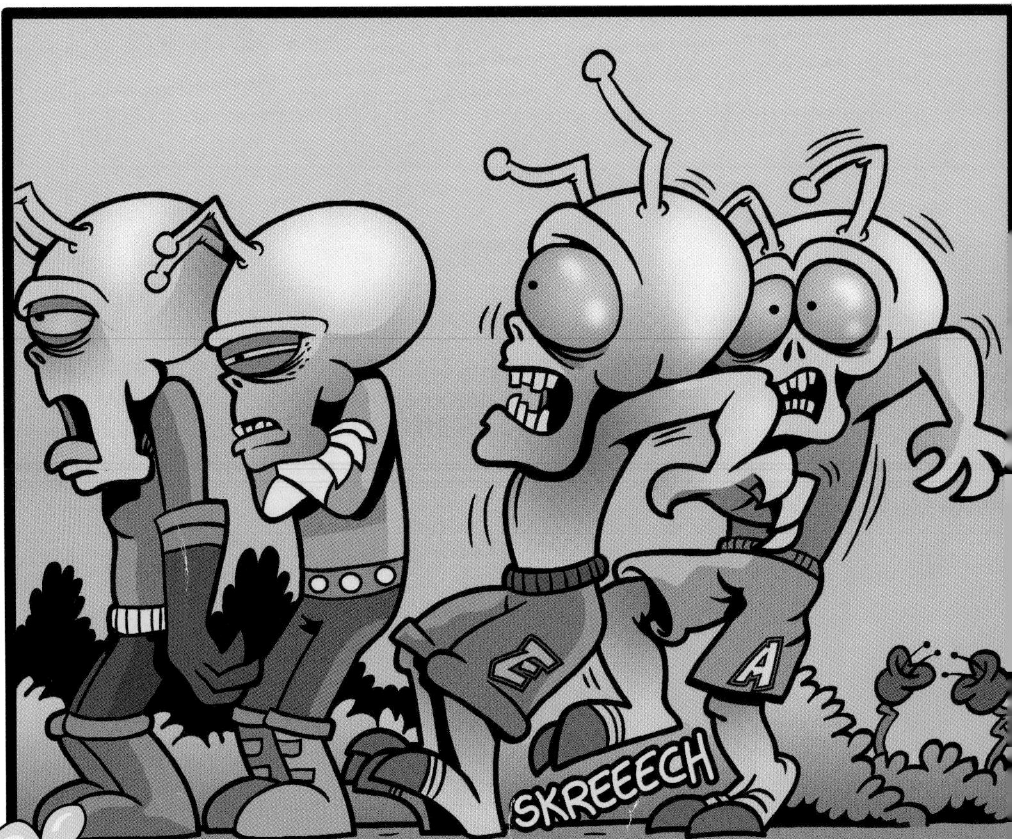
SKREEECH

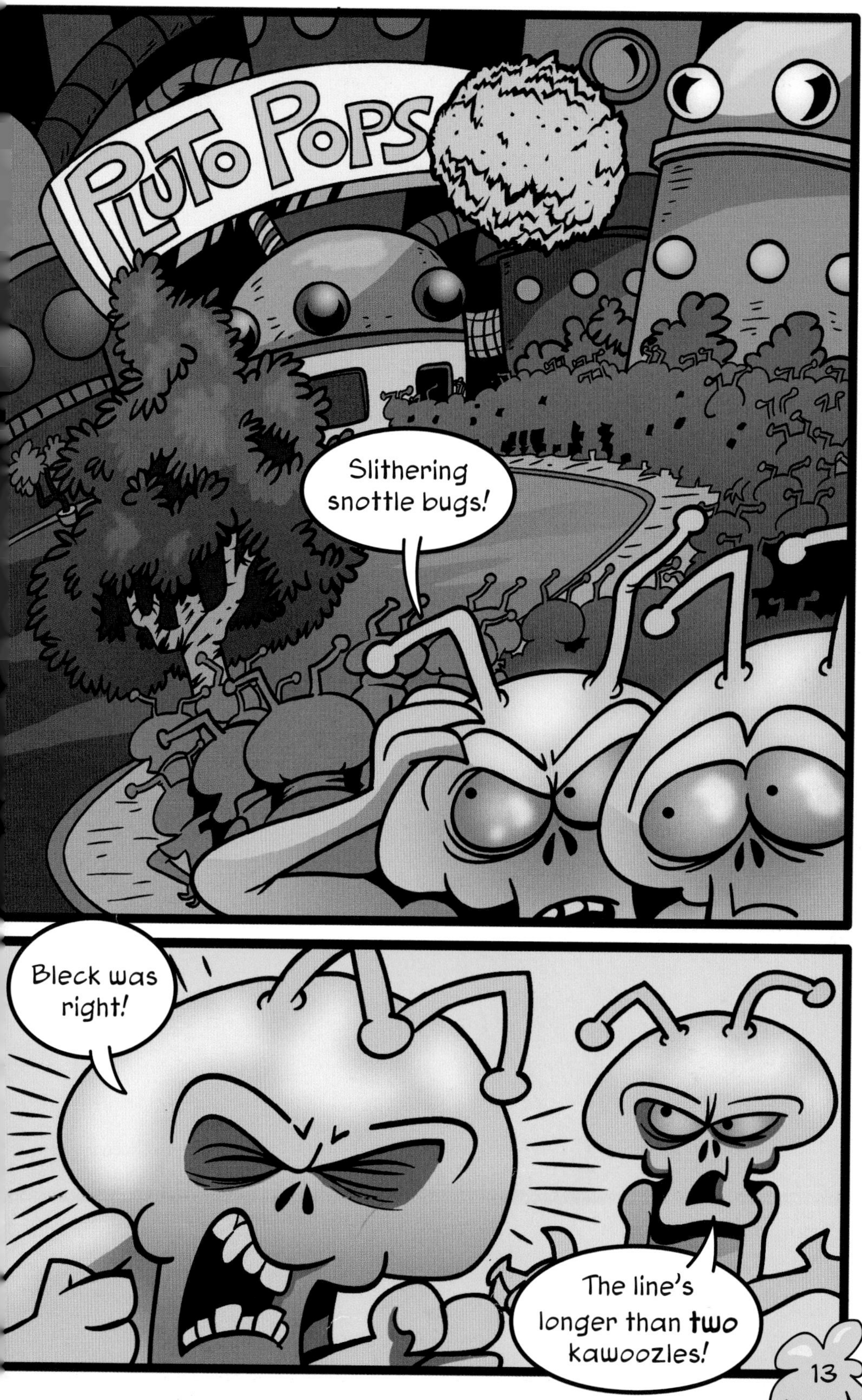
PLUTO POPS
Slithering snottle bugs!
Bleck was right!
The line's longer than **two** kawoozles!

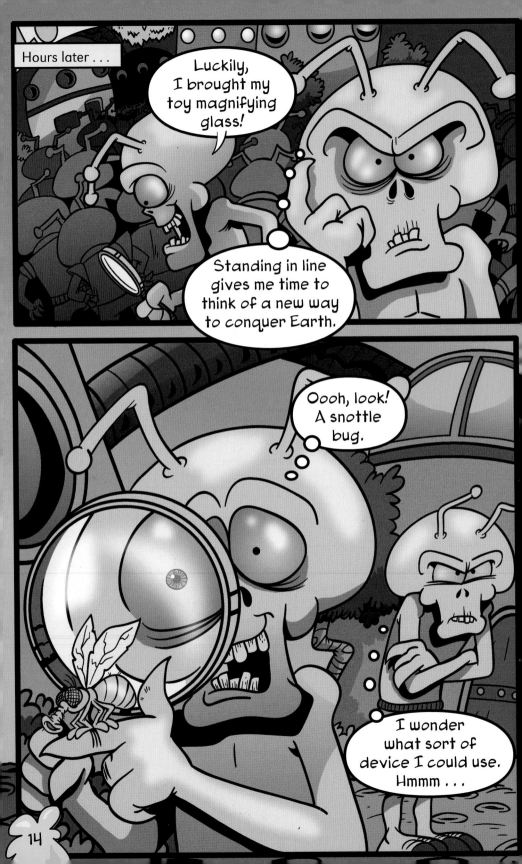

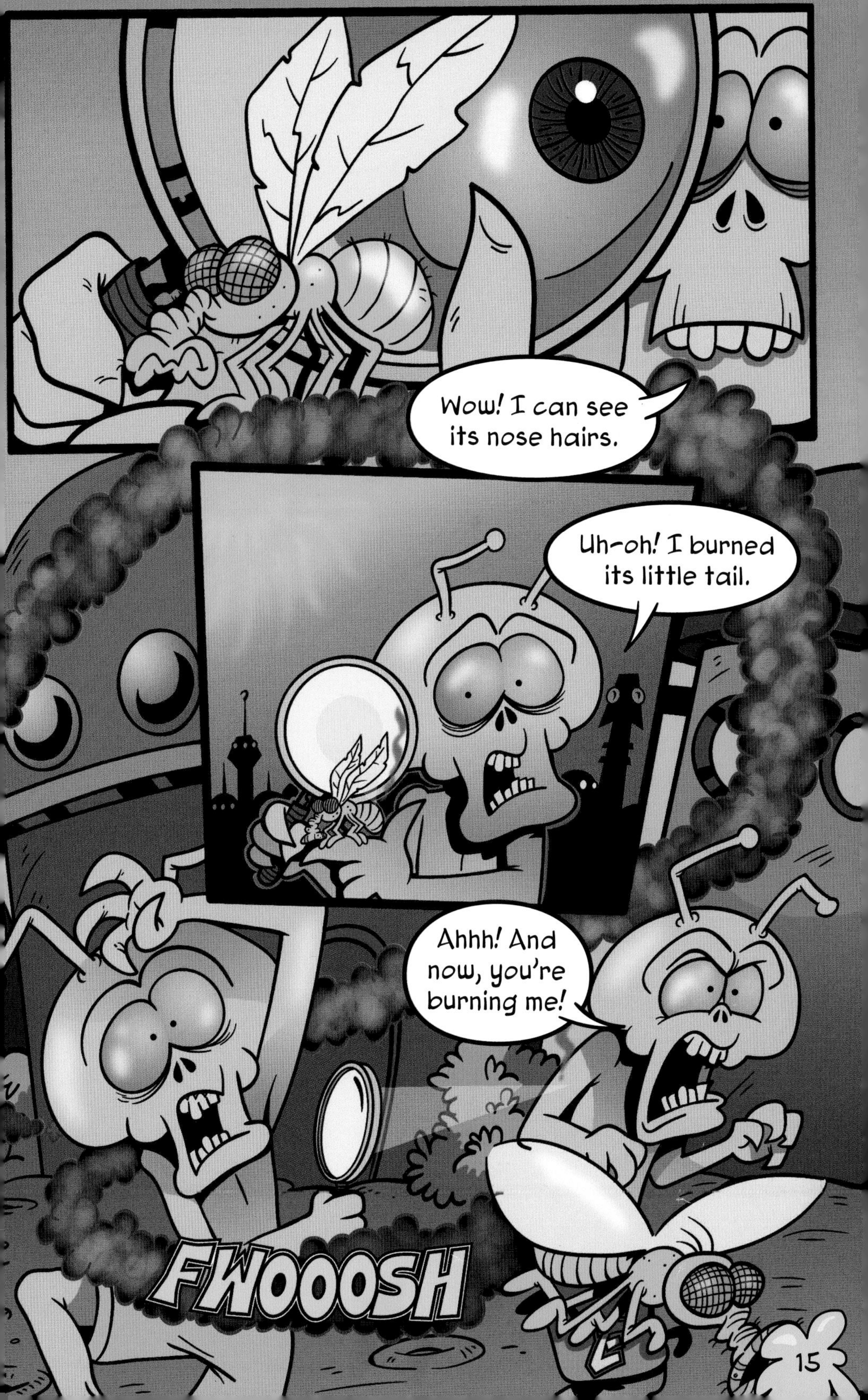
Wow! I can see its nose hairs.
Uh-oh! I burned its little tail.
Ahhh! And now, you're burning me!
FWOOOSH

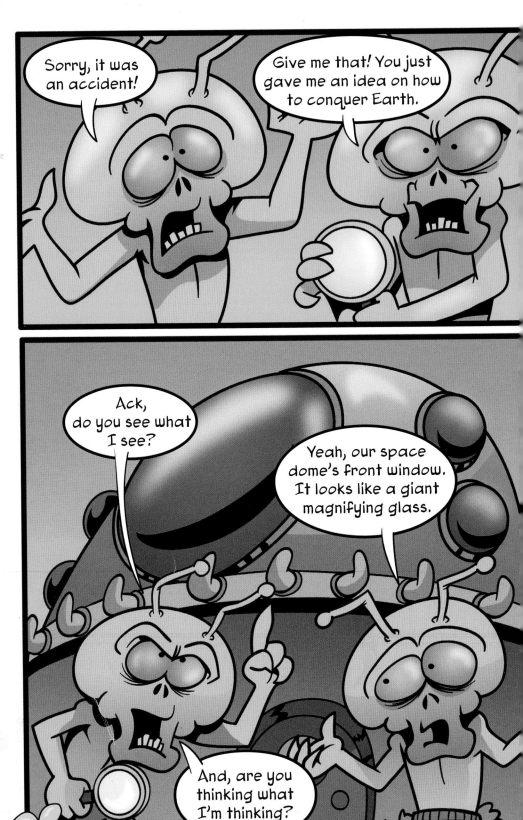

17

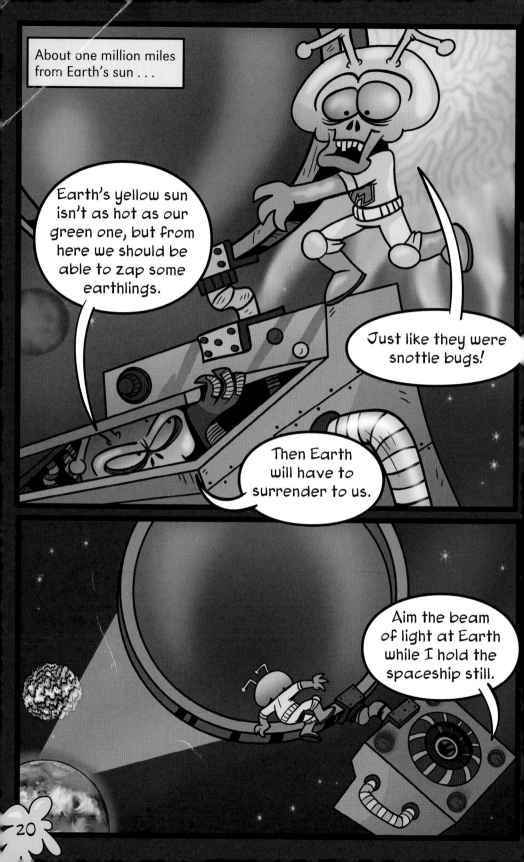

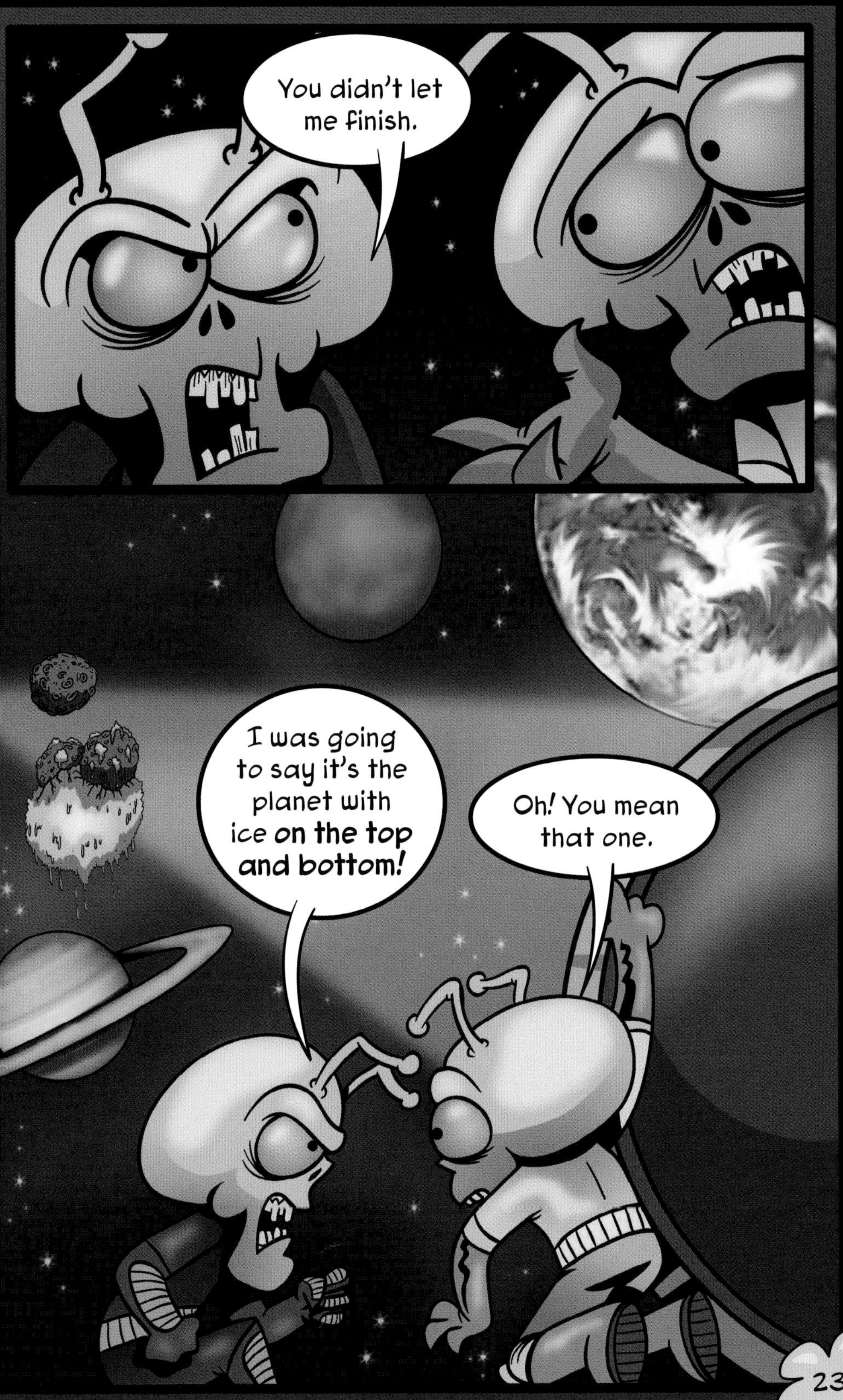
You didn't let me finish.
I was going to say it's the planet with ice **on the top and bottom!**
Oh! You mean that one.

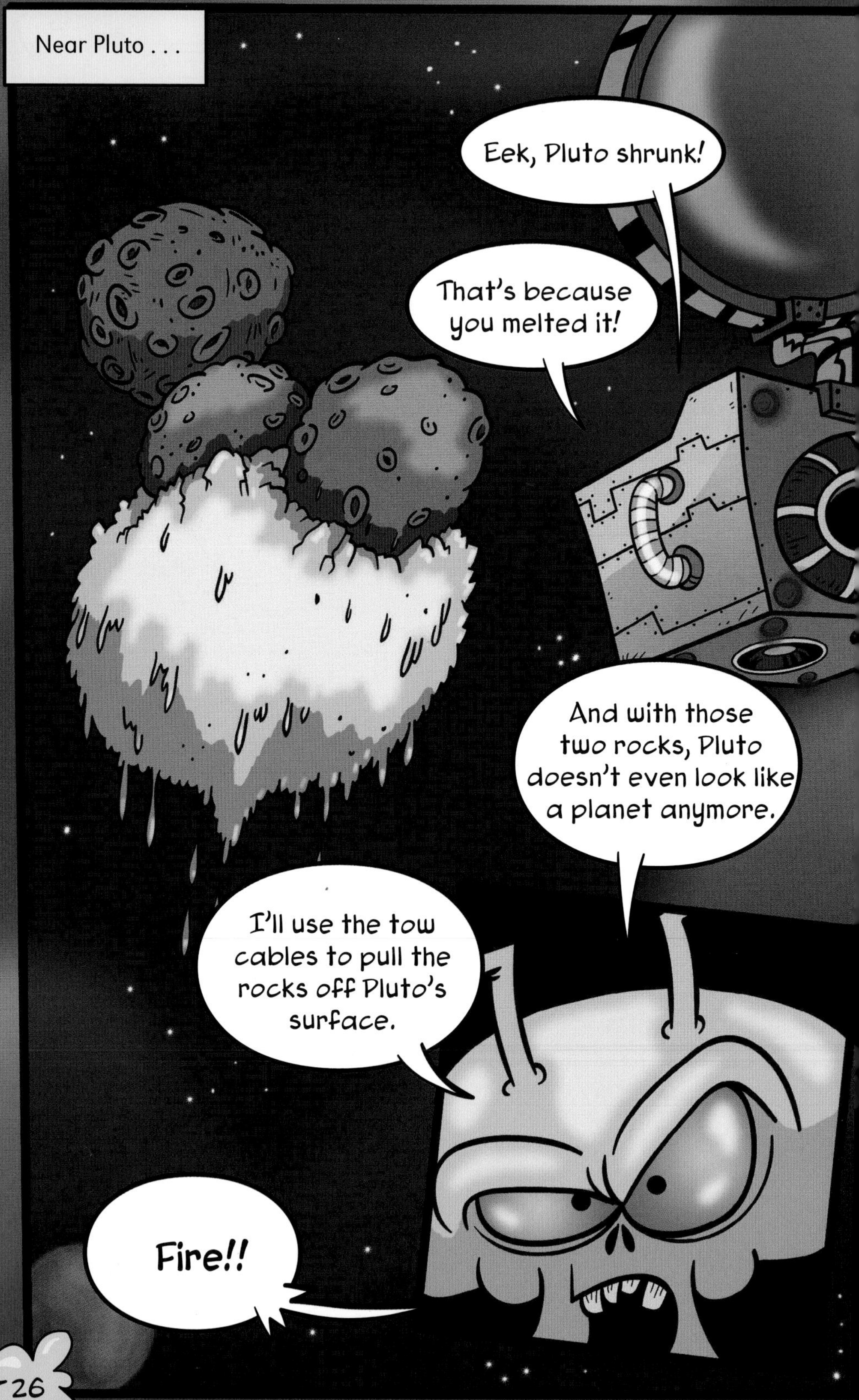
Near Pluto . . .
Eek, Pluto shrunk!
That's because you melted it!
And with those two rocks, Pluto doesn't even look like a planet anymore.
I'll use the tow cables to pull the rocks off Pluto's surface.
Fire!!

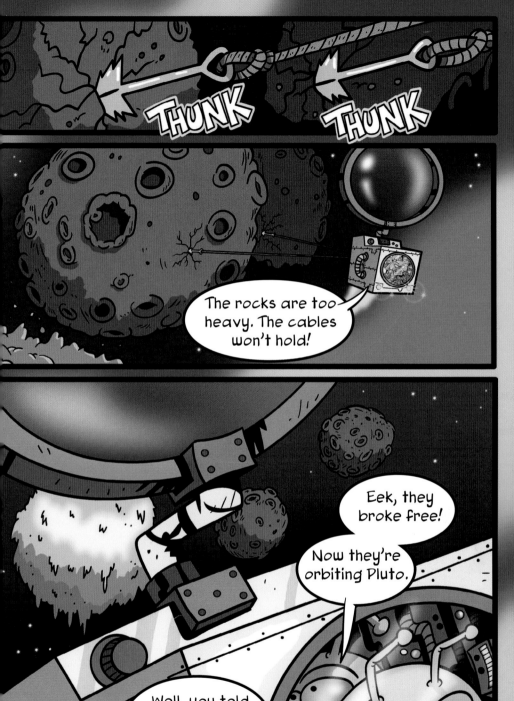

29

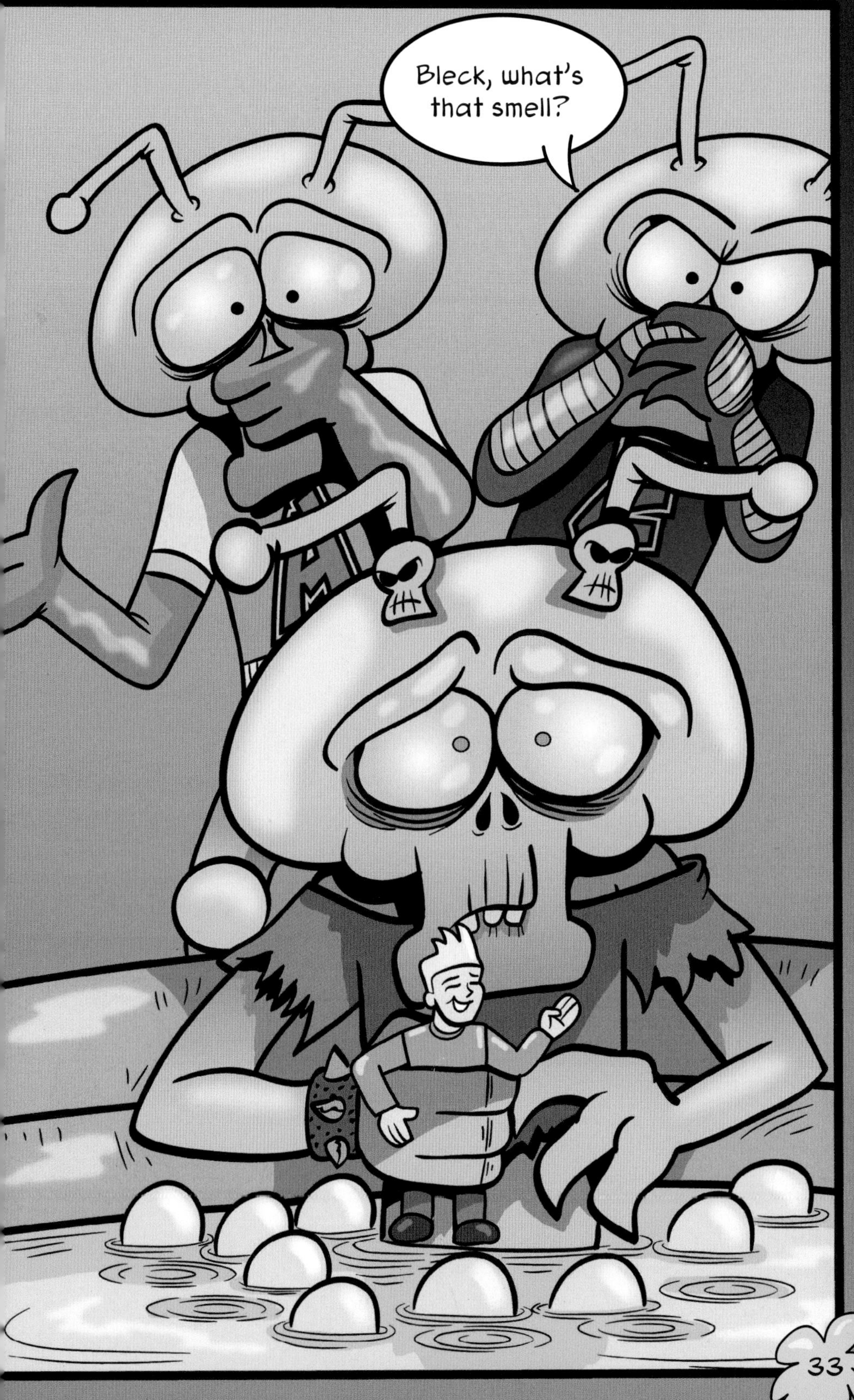
Bleck, what's that smell?

ABOUT THE AUTHOR

Blake A. Hoena once spent a whole weekend just watching his favorite science-fiction movies. Those movies made him wonder what kind of aliens, with their death rays and hyper-drives, couldn't actually conquer Earth. That's when he created Eek and Ack, who play at conquering Earth like earthling kids play at stopping bad guys. Blake has written more than 20 books for children, and currently lives in Minneapolis, Minnesota.

ABOUT THE ILLUSTRATOR

Steve Harpster has loved to draw funny cartoons, mean monsters, and goofy gadgets since he was able to pick up a pencil. In first grade, he avoided writing assignments by working on the pictures for stories instead. Steve was able to land a job drawing funny pictures for books, and that's really what he's best at. Steve lives in Columbus, Ohio, with his wonderful wife, Karen, and their sheepdog, Doodle.

GLOSSARY

action figures (AK-shuhn FIG-yurz)—toys that boys play with; some people mistake them for dolls, but they're not dolls!

astronomer (uh-STRON-uh-muhr)—a scientist who spends a lot of time studying planets, stars, and other stuff in outer space

Einstein (EYEN-styn)—one of the few earthlings that Gloopers (people from the planet Gloop) consider smart

kawoozle (kah-WOOZ-uhl)—a very long, thin creature that lives on the planet Gloop; kawoozles have a body like a snake, but instead of scales, they have sponge-like skin, which picks up dirt and mud as they crawl along the ground, thus the saying "dirty kawoozle". Kawoozles can grow to be an Earth-mile long.

sinister plot (SIN-uh-stur PLOT)—an evil plan, such as zapping earthlings with a giant magnifying glass

telescope (TEL-uh-skope)—an instrument that makes things that are far away look closer and larger, such as stars, planets, and flying washing machines, um, we mean spaceships

FACTS FROM BEYOND

American astronomer Clyde Tombaugh discovered Pluto in 1930.

Eleven-year-old Venetia Burney from Great Britain suggested that Tombaugh's discovery be called Pluto, after the Roman god of the Underworld.

Charon (KARE-on), Pluto's largest moon, was discovered in 1978 by American astronomer James Christy. Its smaller moons, Nix and Hydra, were discovered in 2005 with the Hubble Space Telescope.

Pluto is now called a dwarf planet. Astronomers consider Pluto a dwarf planet because of its small size, and because it shares an orbit with other large objects, such as asteroids. True planets don't share their orbits with other large objects.